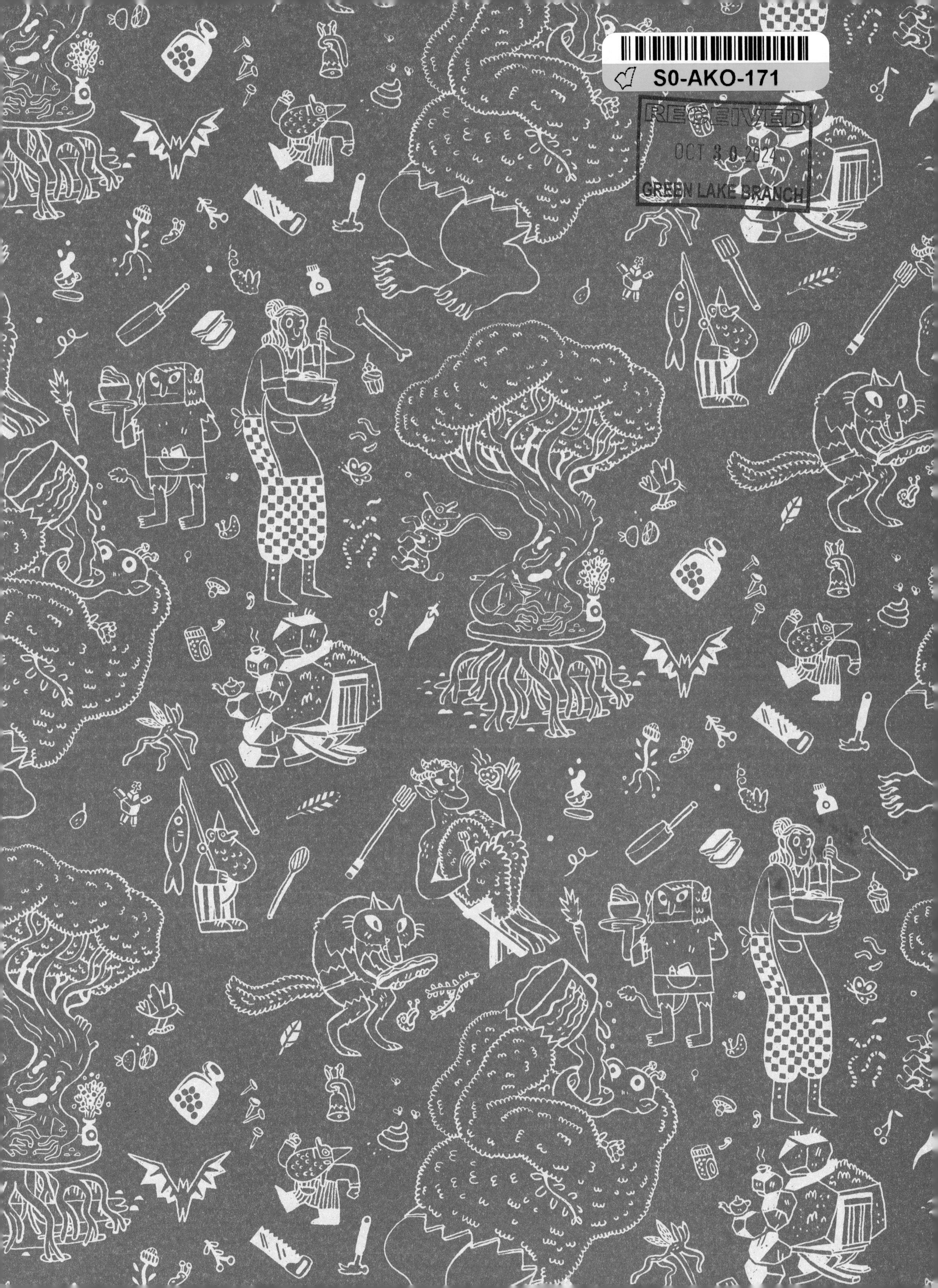

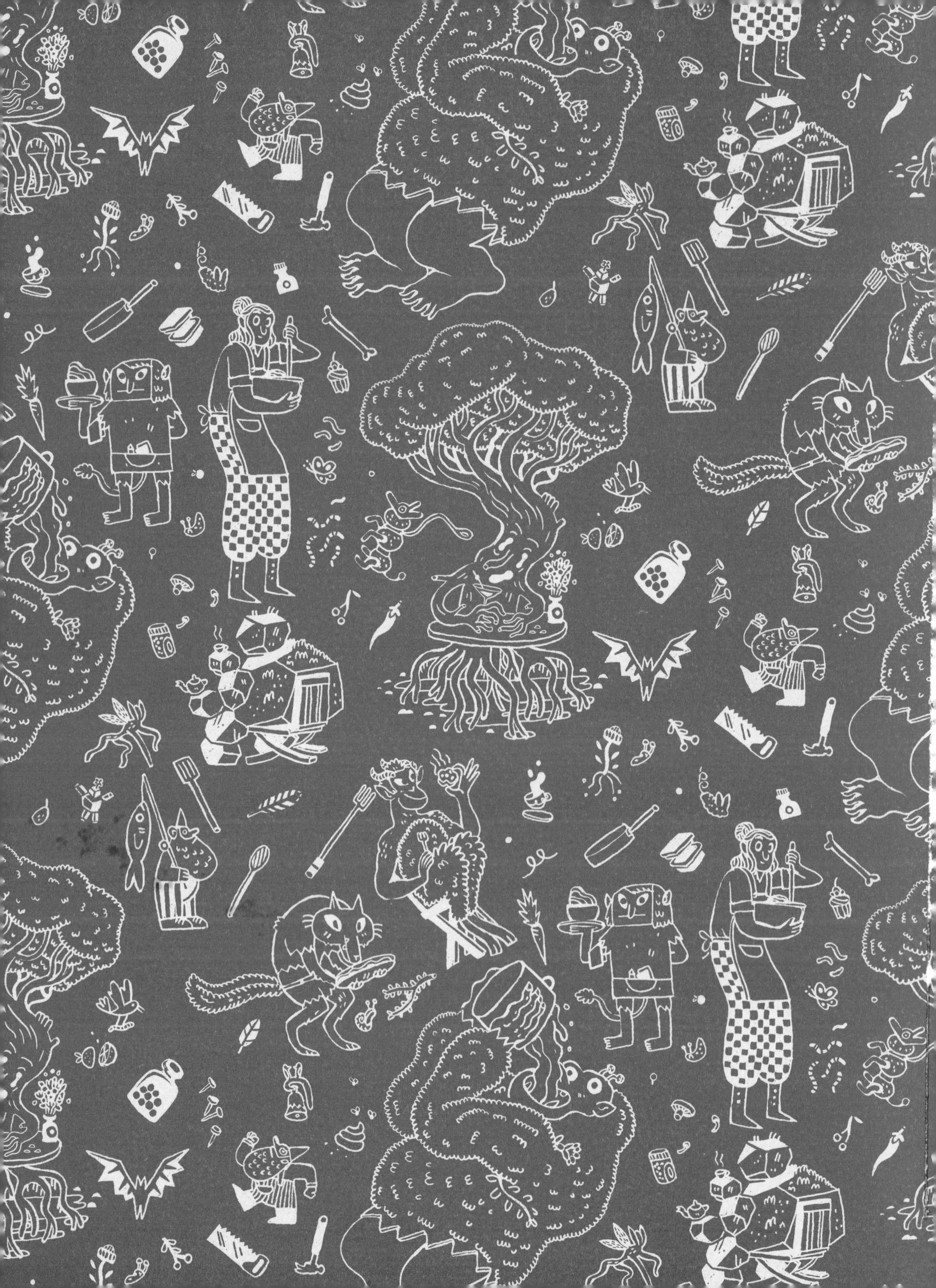

for
JESSICA
& AXEL

Thank you —
Luke Ingram, Alice Blacker, Candice Turvey, Jon Klassen, Robert Hunter,
Gina Glover, Geof Rayner, Caroline Waterlow, and Peter Please.
—M.P.

The Café at the Edge of the Woods
Copyright © 2024 by Mikey Please
All rights reserved. Manufactured in Italy.
No part of this book may be used or reproduced in any manner whatsoever without written
permission except in the case of brief quotations embodied in critical articles and reviews. For
information address HarperCollins Children's Books, a division of HarperCollins Publishers,
195 Broadway, New York, NY 10007.
www.harpercollinschildrens.com

Library of Congress Control Number: 2023944815
ISBN 978-0-06-334549-2

24 25 26 27 28 RTLO 10 9 8 7 6 5 4 3 2 1

First U.S. edition, 2024

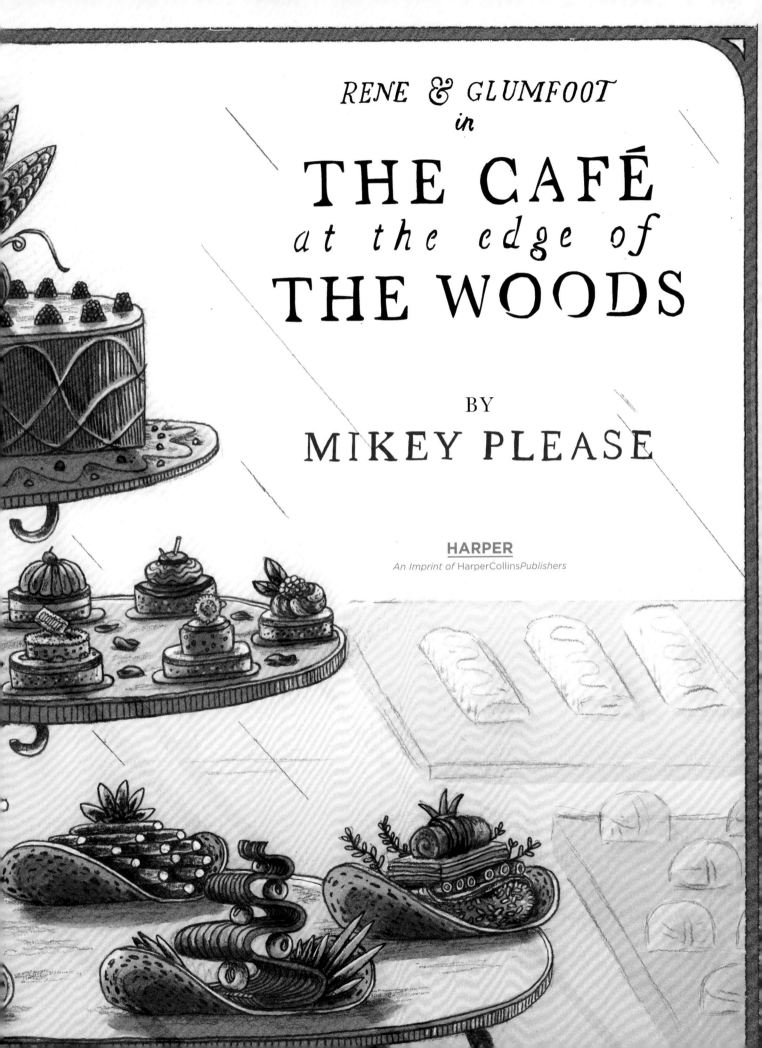

RENE & GLUMFOOT
in

THE CAFÉ
at the edge of
THE WOODS

BY

MIKEY PLEASE

HARPER
An Imprint of HarperCollinsPublishers

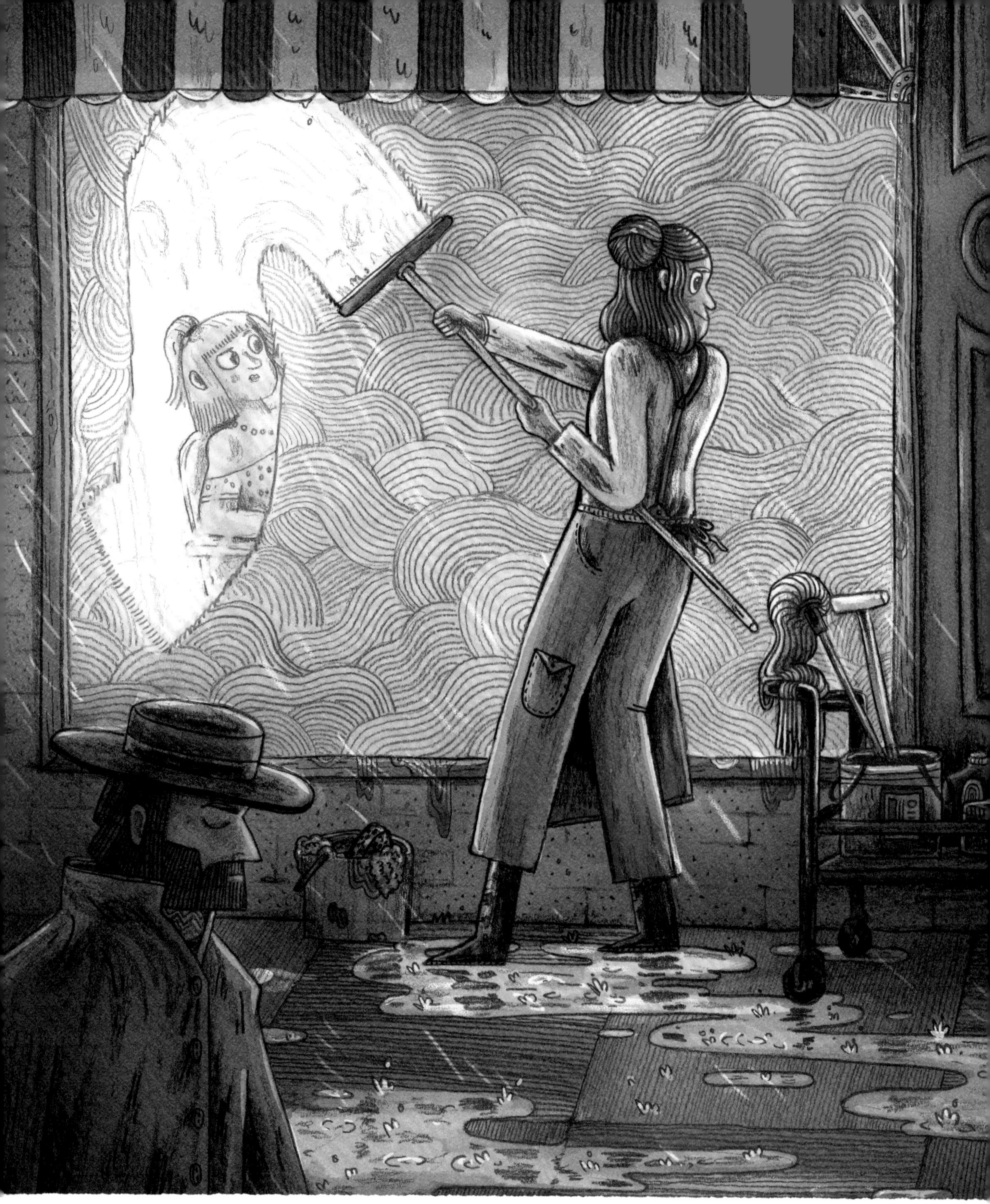

Rene dreamed

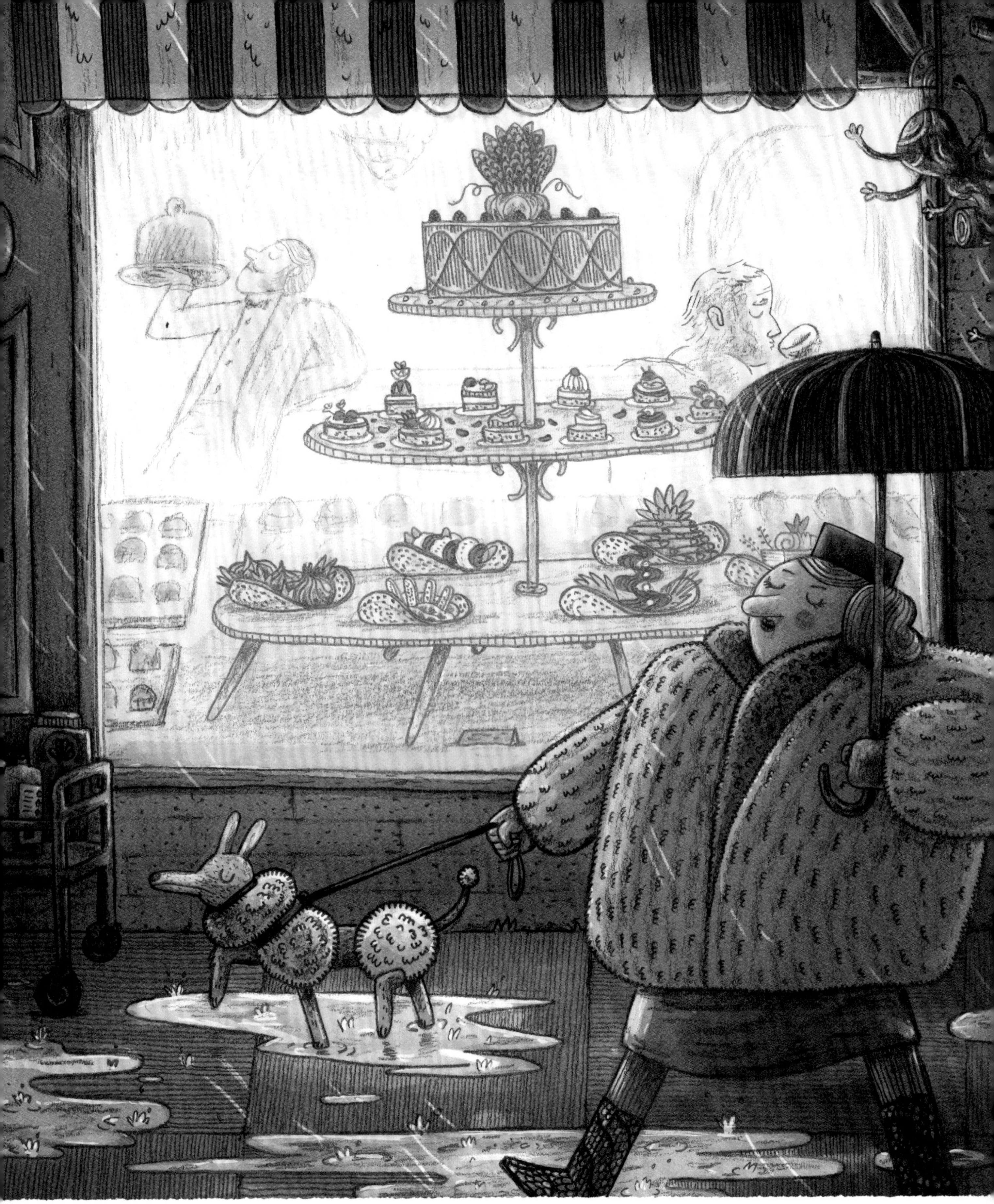

of fine cusine,

and so
she saved up
every bean.

Then built a building
beam by beam—

THE CAFÉ
AT THE EDGE
OF THE WOODS.

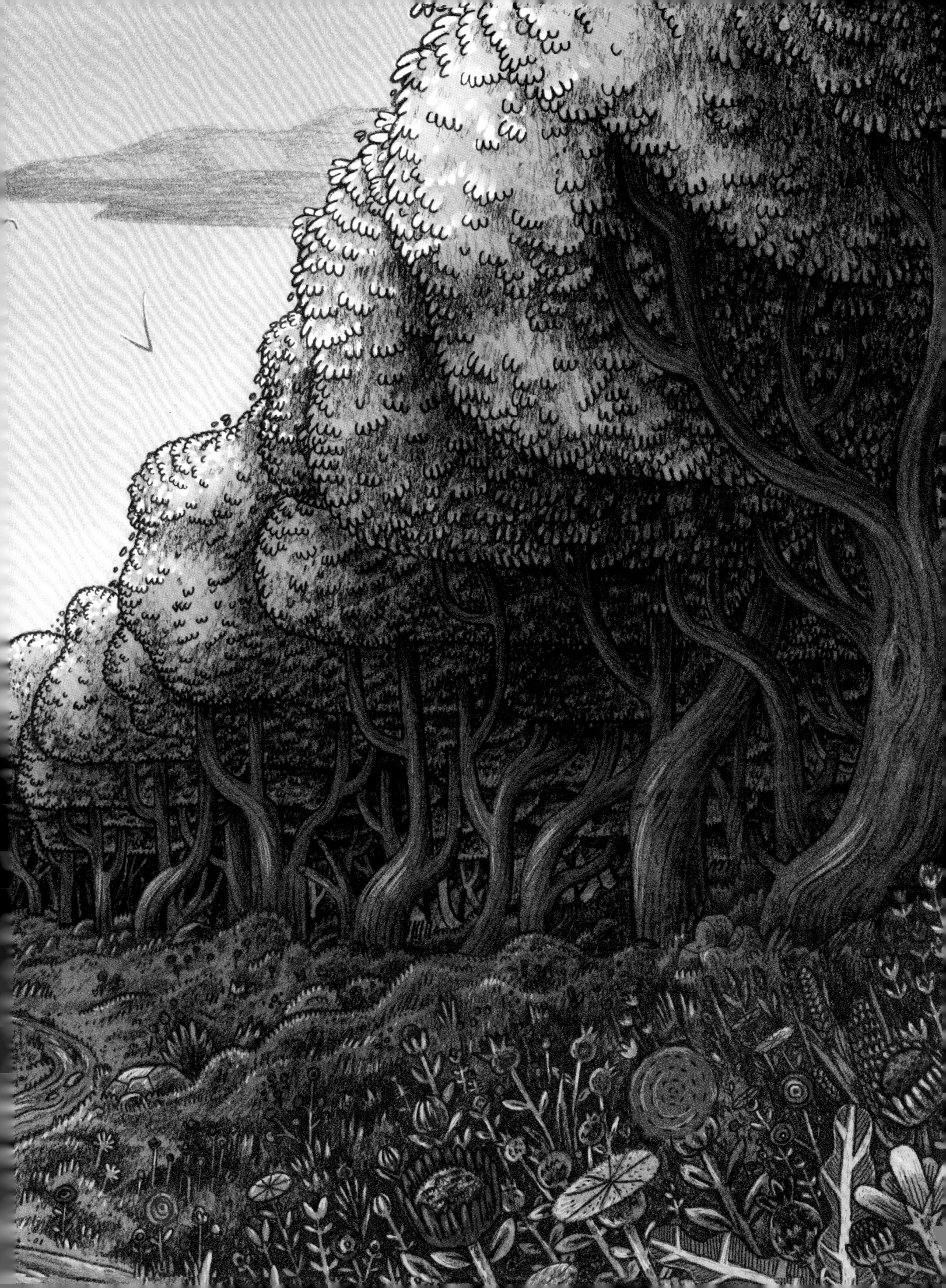

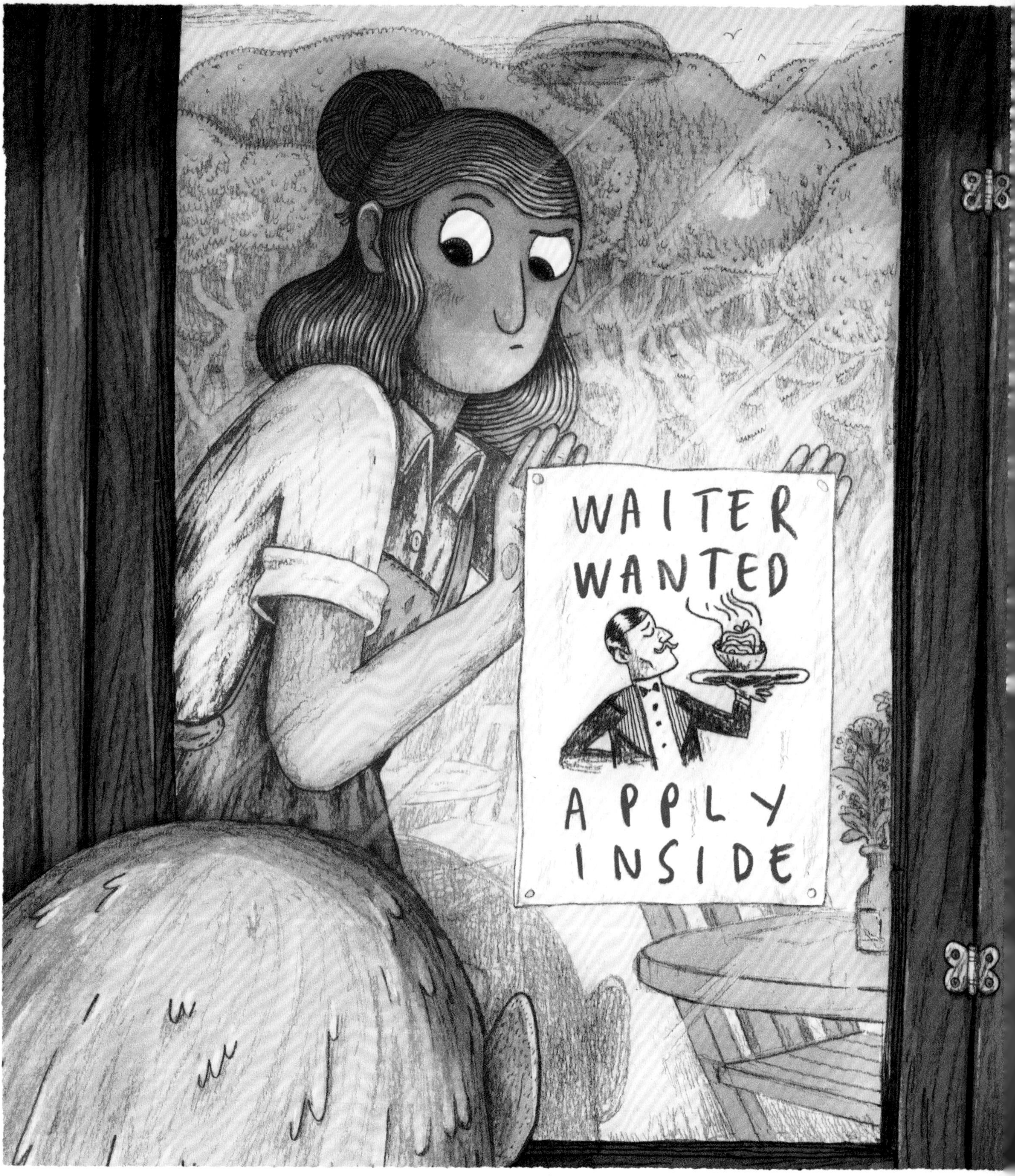
WAITER
WANTED
APPLY
INSIDE

A single applicant replied.
"Suppose you'll do then," Rene sighed.

The waiter's name was **Glumfoot**.

Above the door there hung a bell
to welcome in new clientele.

But every morning silence fell.
No customers came calling.

*"Perhaps this plot
is the worst spot?
A business plan,
I sure had not."*

*"My hopes and dreams
will turn to rot!"*

The waiter
went out walking.

He soon returned with company
who stooped and stumbled clumsily.
The man was taller than a tree.
"A customer!" croaked Glumfoot.

Rene gawped and gasped in awe.

Knuckles dragged upon the floor.

Tusks stuck from a lower jaw.

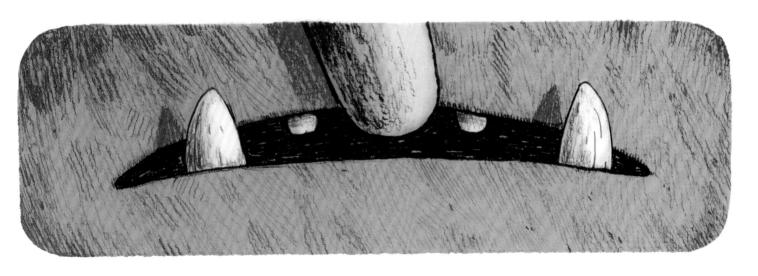

The customer was . . .

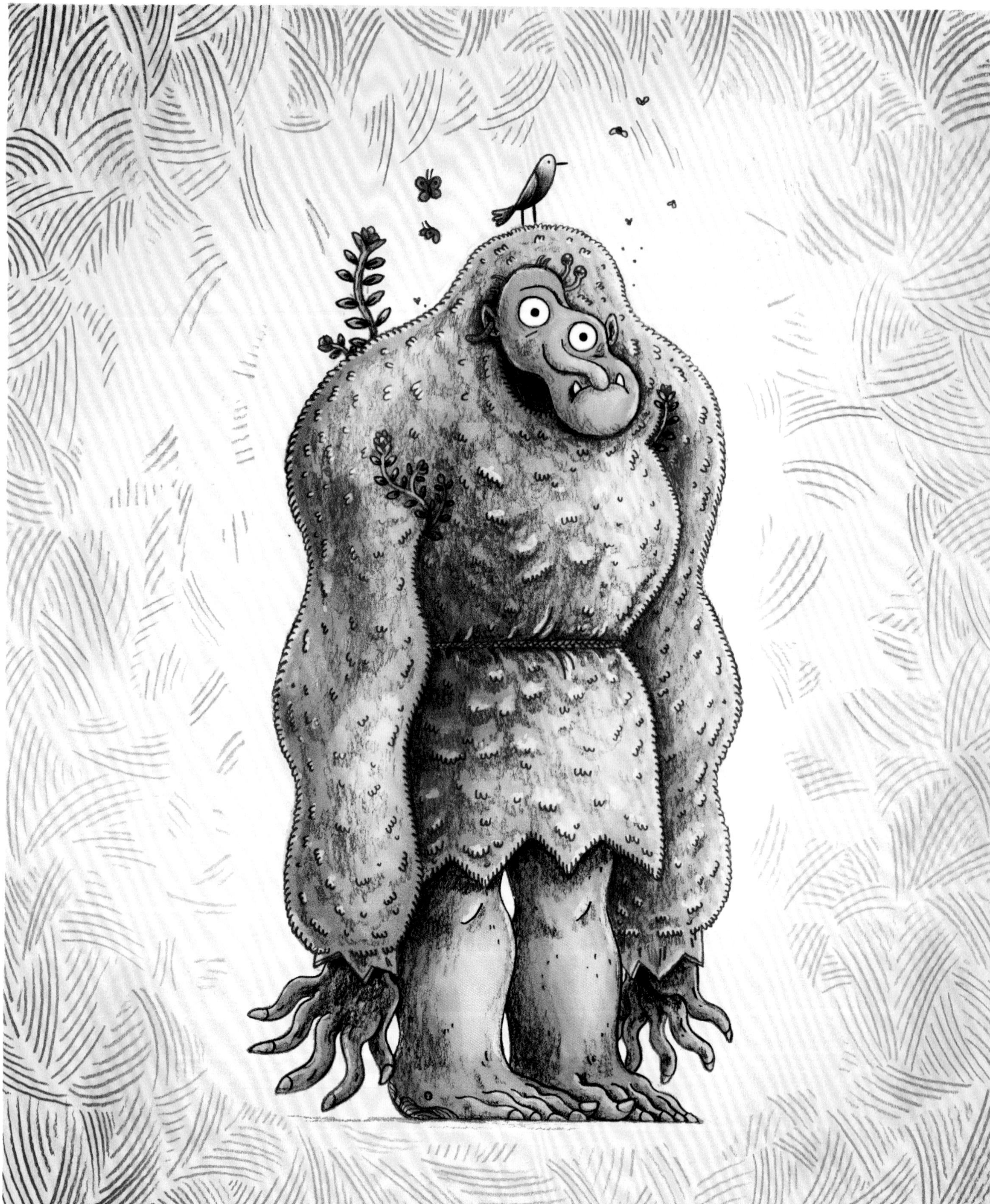

an Ogre.

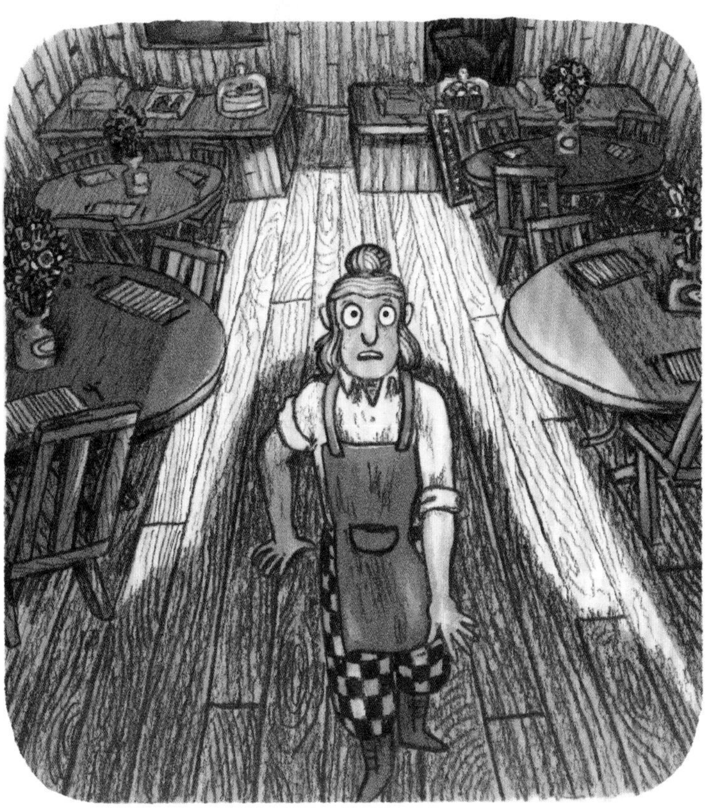

"Ah . . .

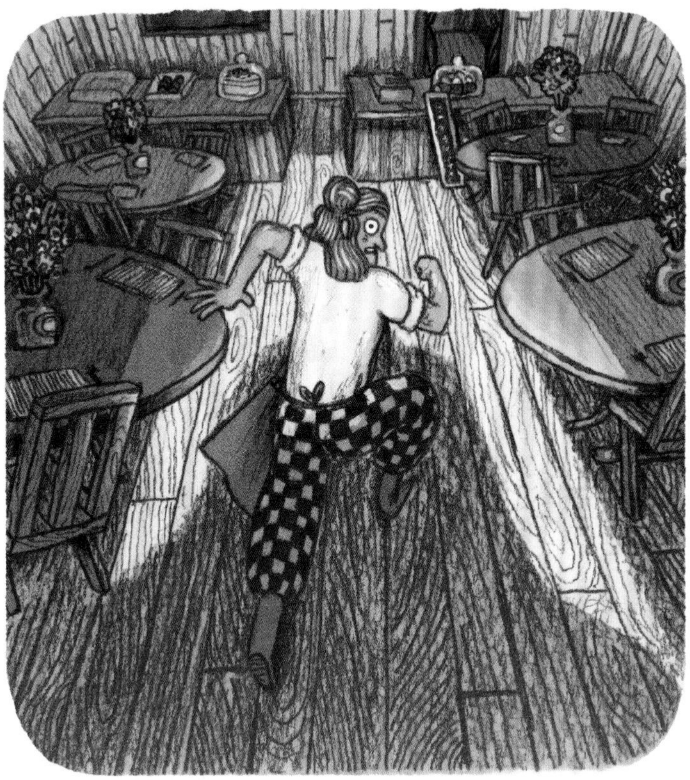

Ah . . .

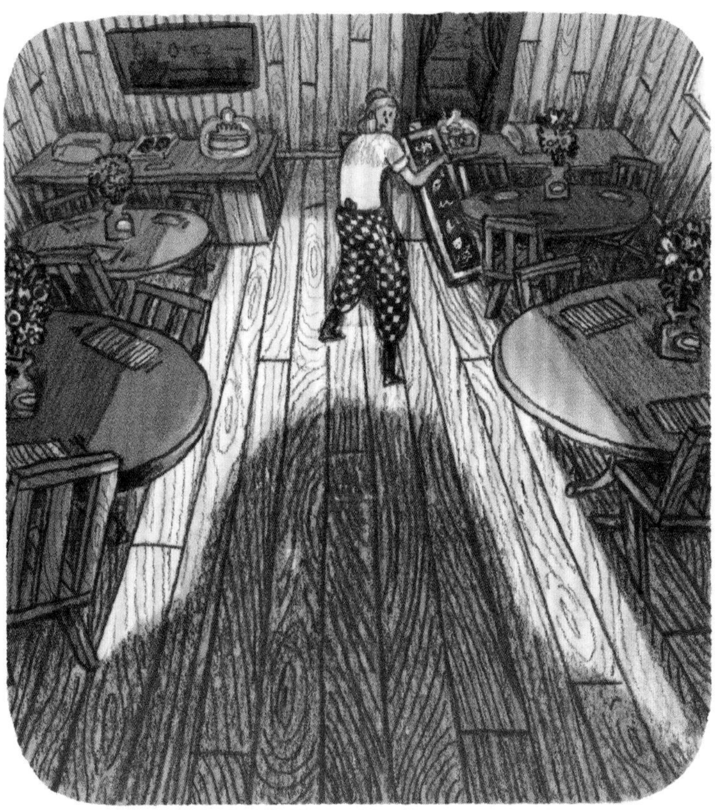

Ah . . .

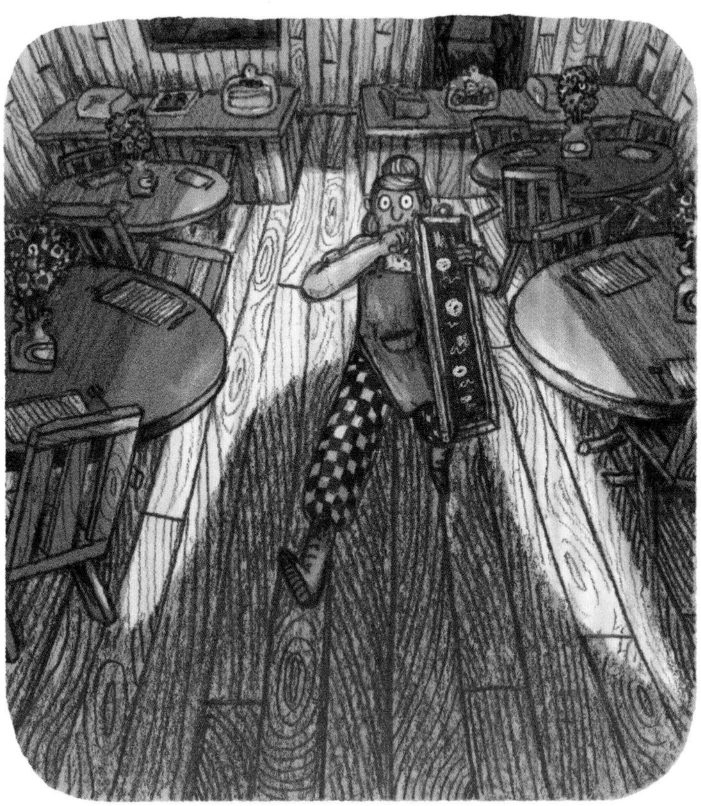

A-hem!"

"*Today's special is gravlax
with saffron sautéed sticklebacks.*"

"I'll grab a bag
of pickled BATS."

"Pickled whats?"
said Rene.

*"The truffle stew
is rather nice.
It comes with peas
and long grain rice."*

"Bats! And slugs and battered mice!"

"Slugs and mice?!"
gasped Rene.

"Perhaps you'd like the cheddar tart?
Topped with chopped artichoke heart."

"A bag of bats! That smells like fart!"

"*Smells like WHAT?!*" shrieked Rene.

"*That is it! No more! I've had enough.*
I won't serve such disgusting stuff!"
Rene stormed off in a huff.

"One moment, sir," said Glumfoot.

"I knew this was an awful plan.
Pack my porcelain and pan.
Glumfoot, fetch a moving van."
The waiter leaned and whispered . . .

"The ogre's had a change of heart. He'd love to try the cheddar tart and all the rest. Best make a start— his appetite's enormous."

Rene's hand went to her chest. Her heart was pumping through her vest. *"He'll have nothing but the very best! Glumfoot, fetch the saucepan."*

With fire and oil and swirling blade,
pastry puffed! Mushroom sautéed!
Each dish delicately displayed
on top of Glumfoot's trolley.

But soon as Rene had turned her back,
Glumfoot shuffled this and that,

so when it reached the ogre's mat,
everything looked different.

The tart got flipped
onto its back,

so it looked like
a pickled bat.

The saffron swirls
and sticklebacks

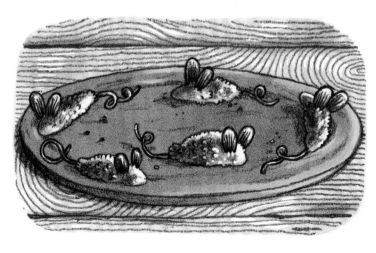

became
the battered mice.

The truffle stew
was shuffled, too

to make it look like
slugs in goo.

The rice became . . .

maggot fondue!
The whole lot looked disgusting.

Rene glanced up
as Glumfoot wheeled
the ogre his gigantic meal.
She held her breath!
Would this appeal?

The ogre looked suspicious.

Then with a ROAR the ogre ate
every scrap on every plate.
He burped and mumbled,
"THAT WAS GREAT."
Rene was delighted.

She burst out of
the kitchen door.
*"You like it?
Would you like some more?"*

"I'd take a plate of that stuff. Your
maggots were delicious."

"*Maggots?!*" On her heel she spun.
"*Glumfoot? Tell. What have you done?*"
Rene turned from peach to plum.
The ogre interrupted—

"I never knew
that slugs could be
so crispy.
yet so tingly.
With subtle hints
of salty sea."

Rene's mouth
hung open.

"And who knew that old bat could taste
nothing like some household waste?"
"That would be the miso paste,"
said Rene, standing straighter.

"Thanks for that.
I'll come again.
And tell my
family and friends.

There's lots of folks
around these ends
who'd like this
sorta litter."

Knuckles dragged towards the door.
A smile creased the tusk-lined jaw.

And on the table Rene saw . . .
a pile of golden nuggets.

"Glumfoot, I've been a nincompoop.
But you've shown me a different route.

*From now on I shall make the soup,
and you shall write the menu.*"

And from that day forth,
above the door,
the bell tinkled
as more and more
creatures from
legend and lore

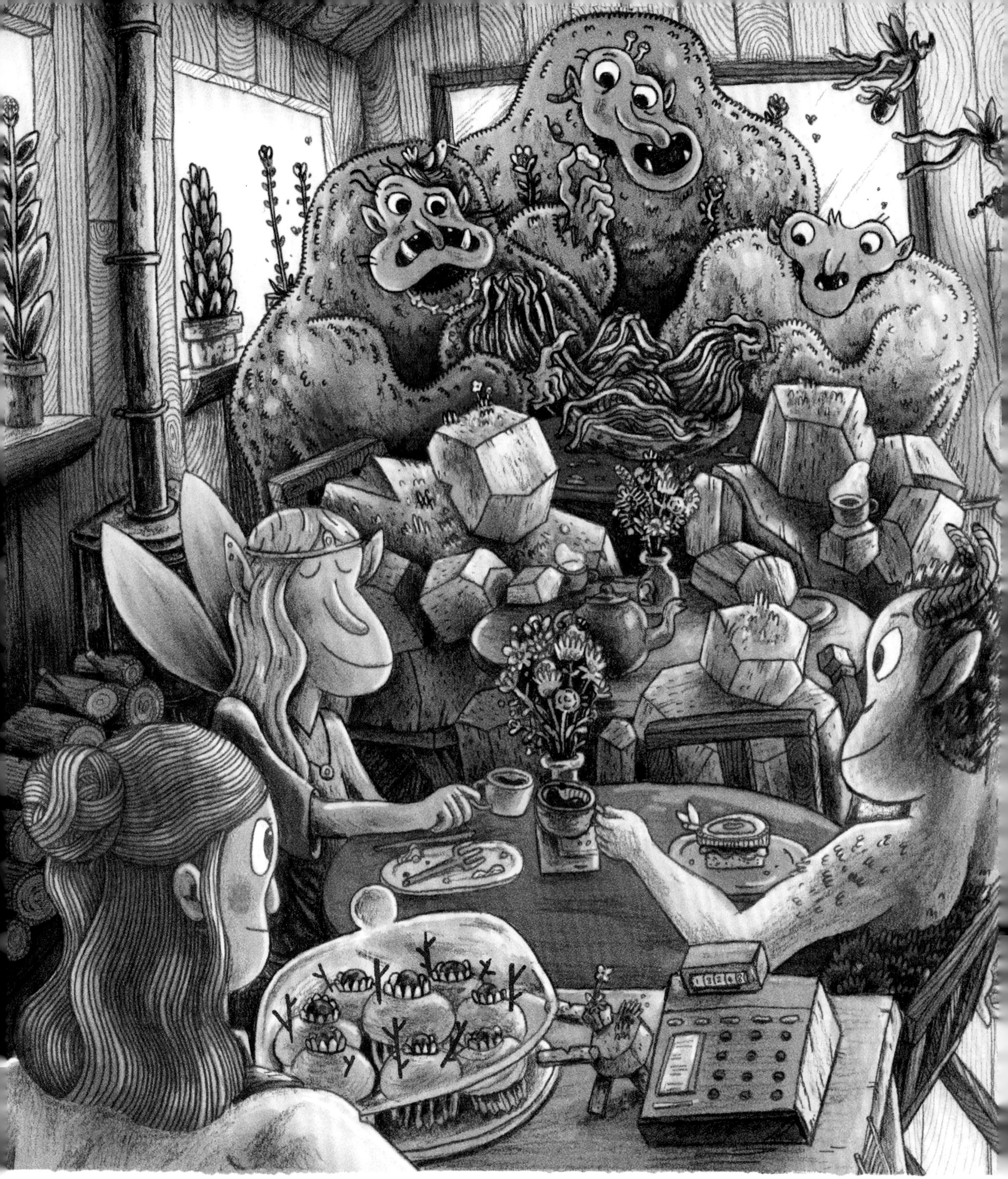

came looking for

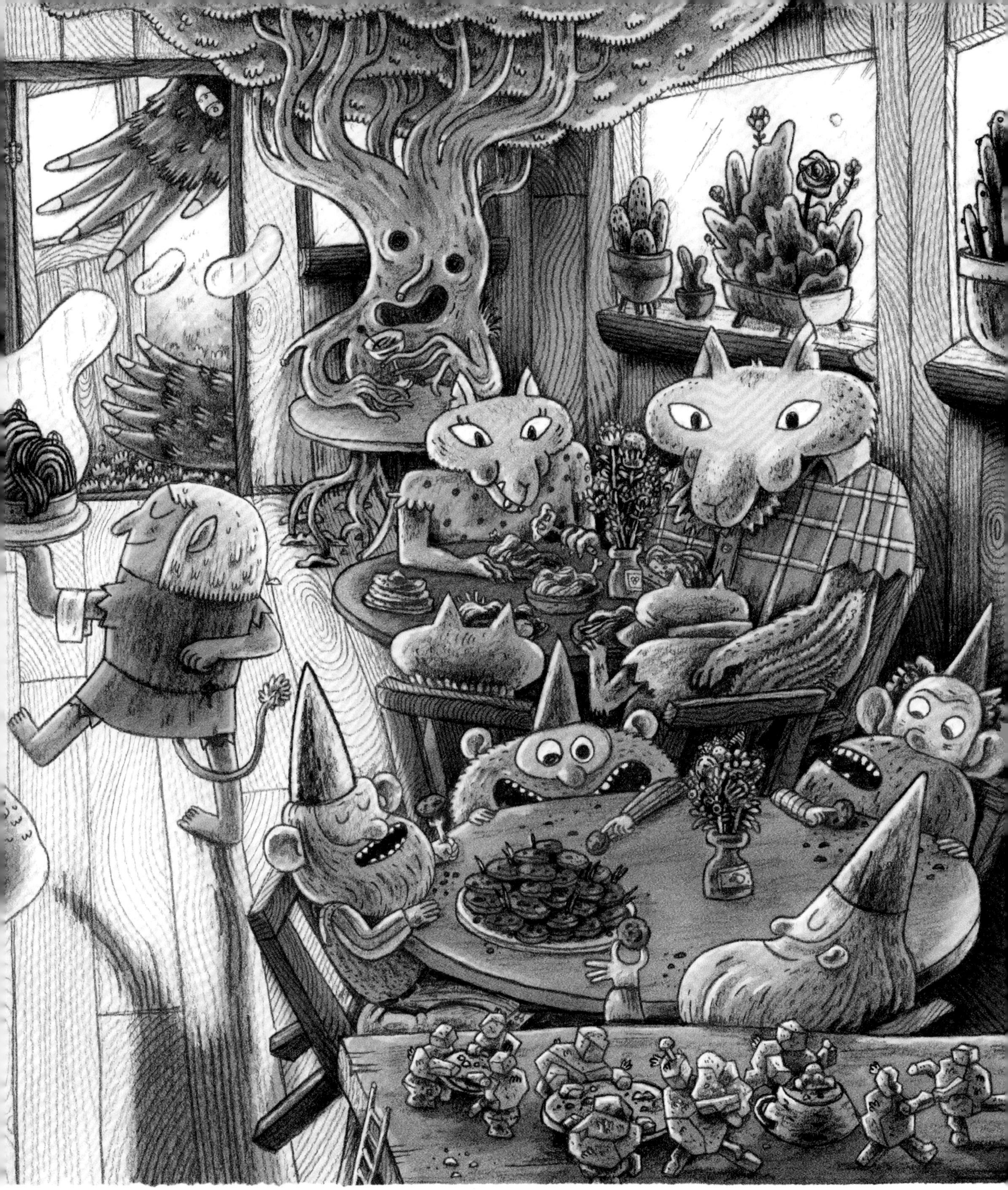

some breakfast.

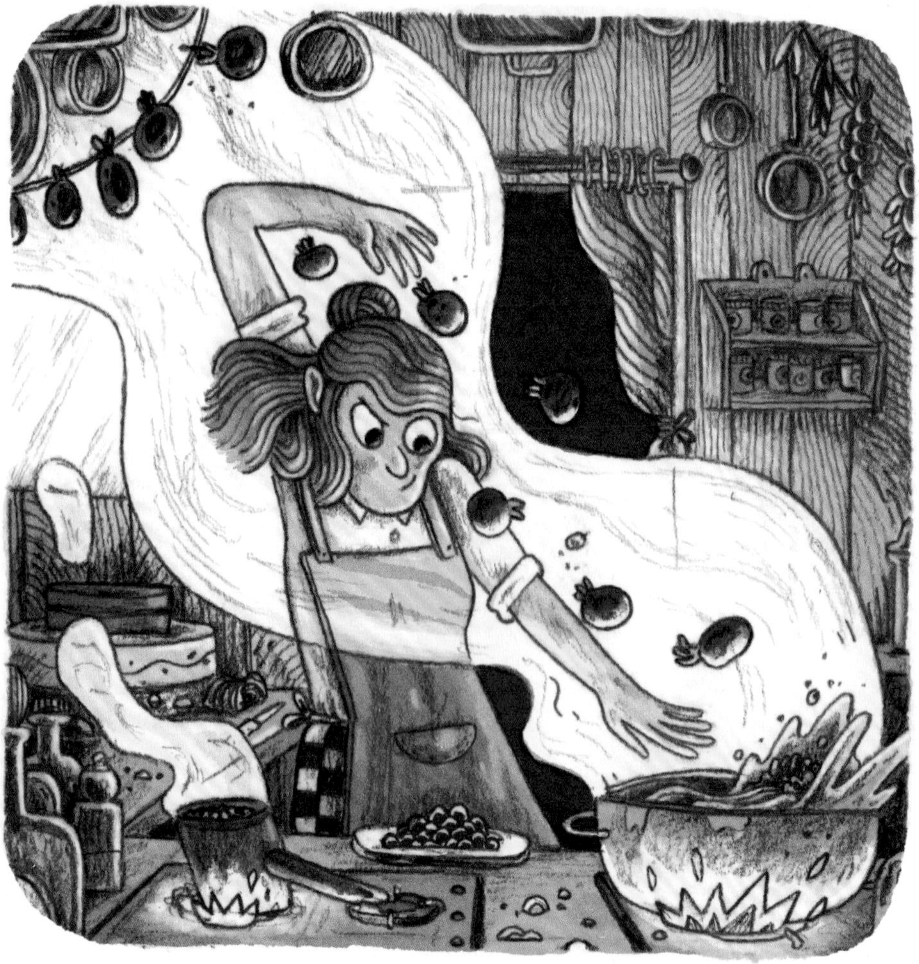

And Rene
cooked up
fine cusine,

while
Glumfoot's
menus
raised
a scream.

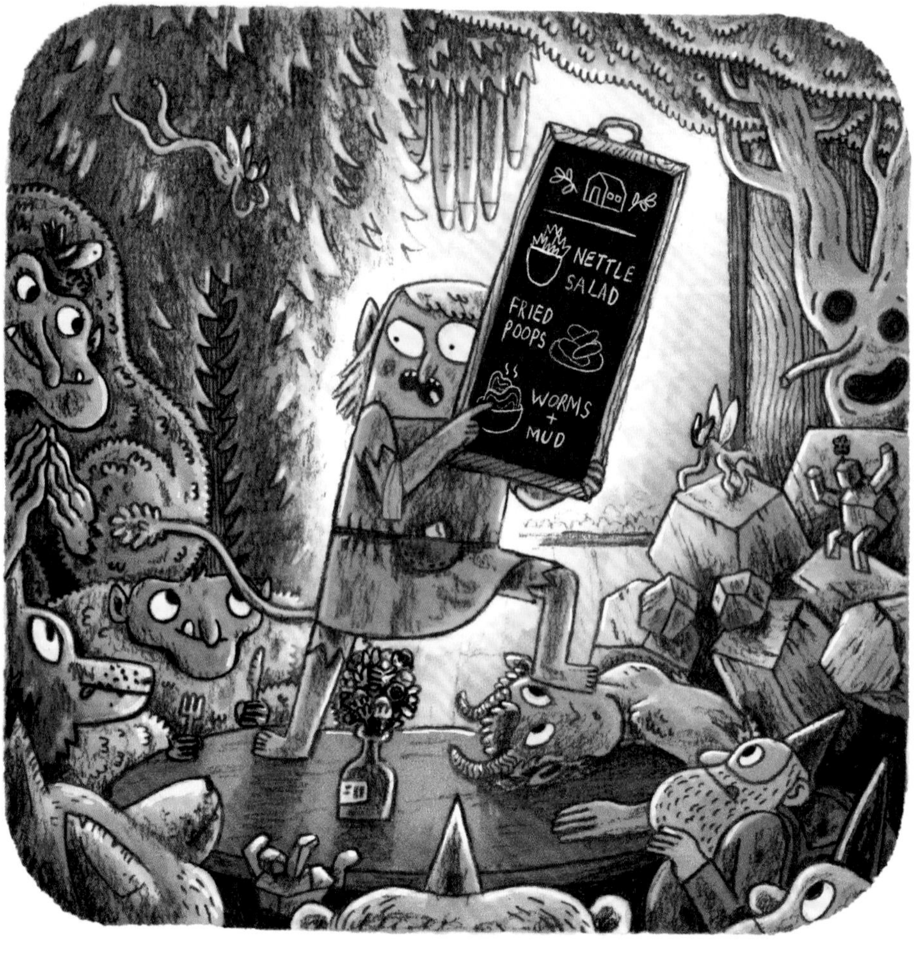
NETTLE SALAD
FRIED POOPS
WORMS + MUD

They truly were the perfect team in . . .

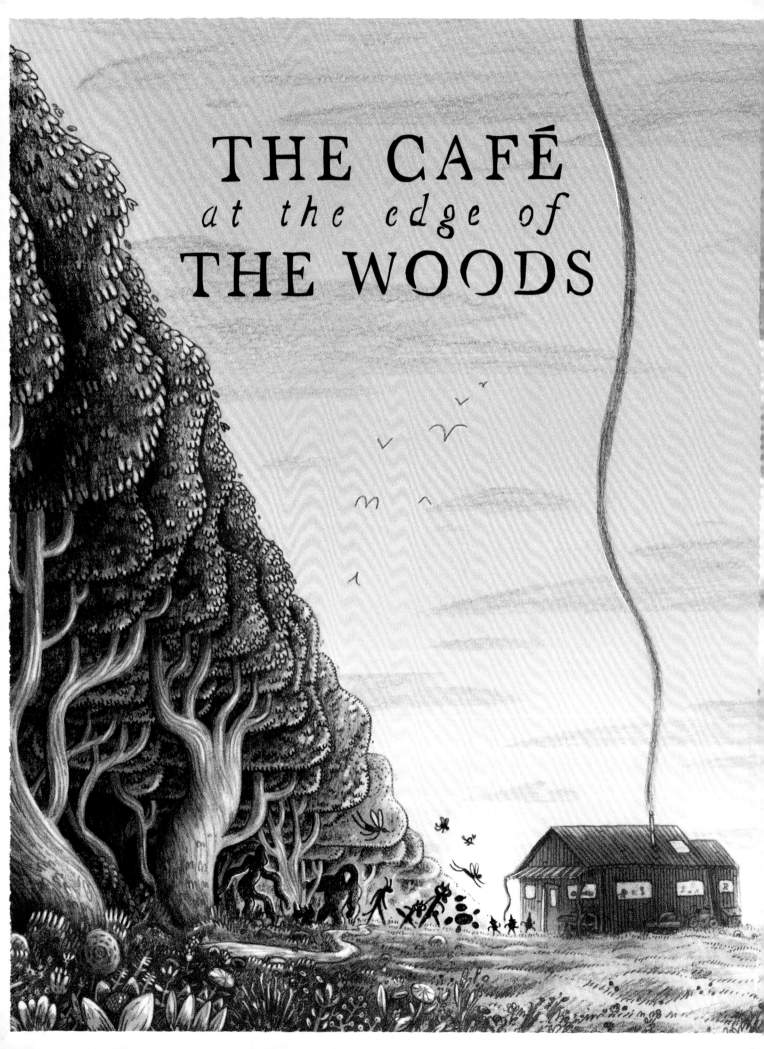

THE CAFÉ
at the edge of
THE WOODS

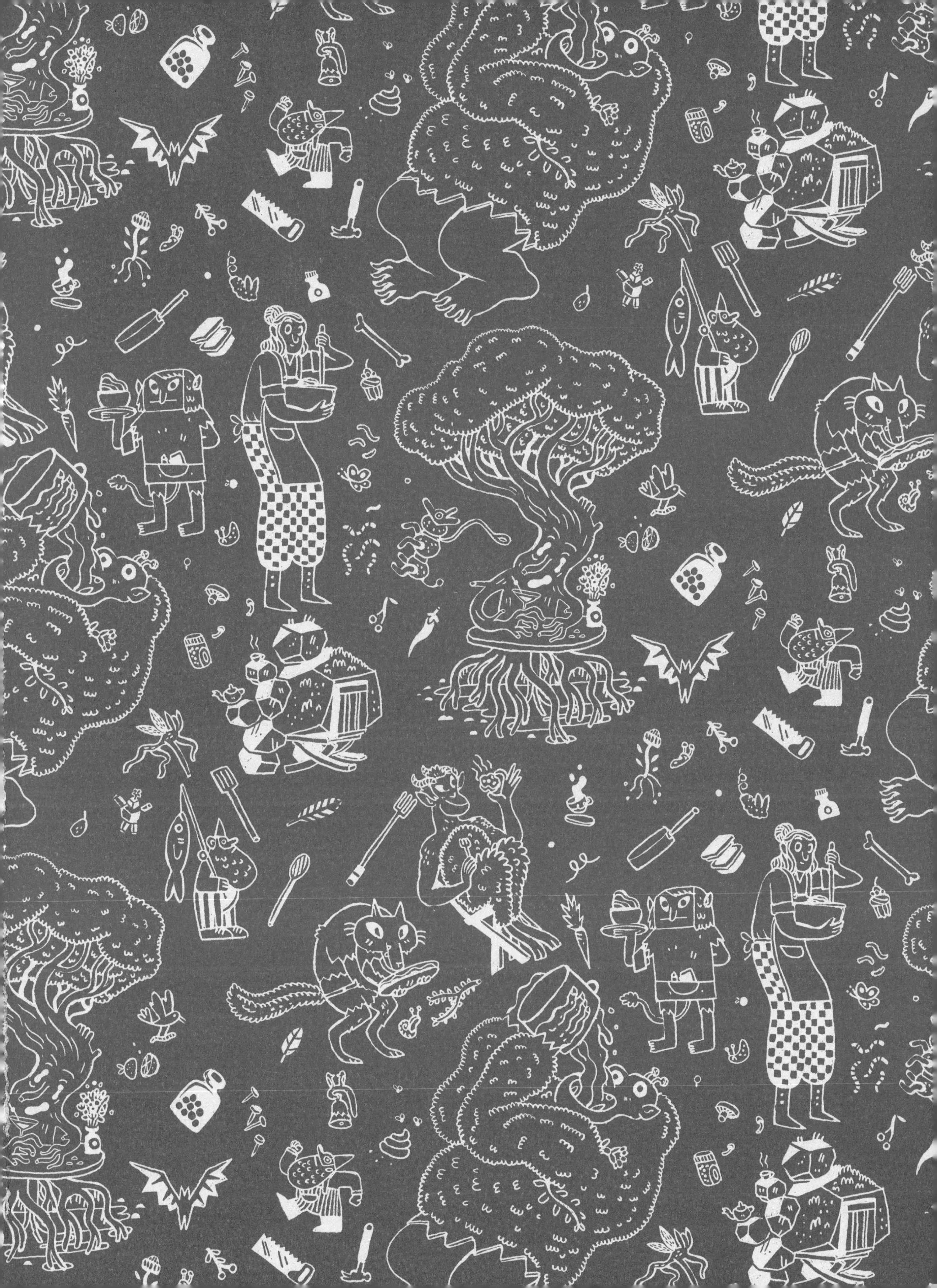

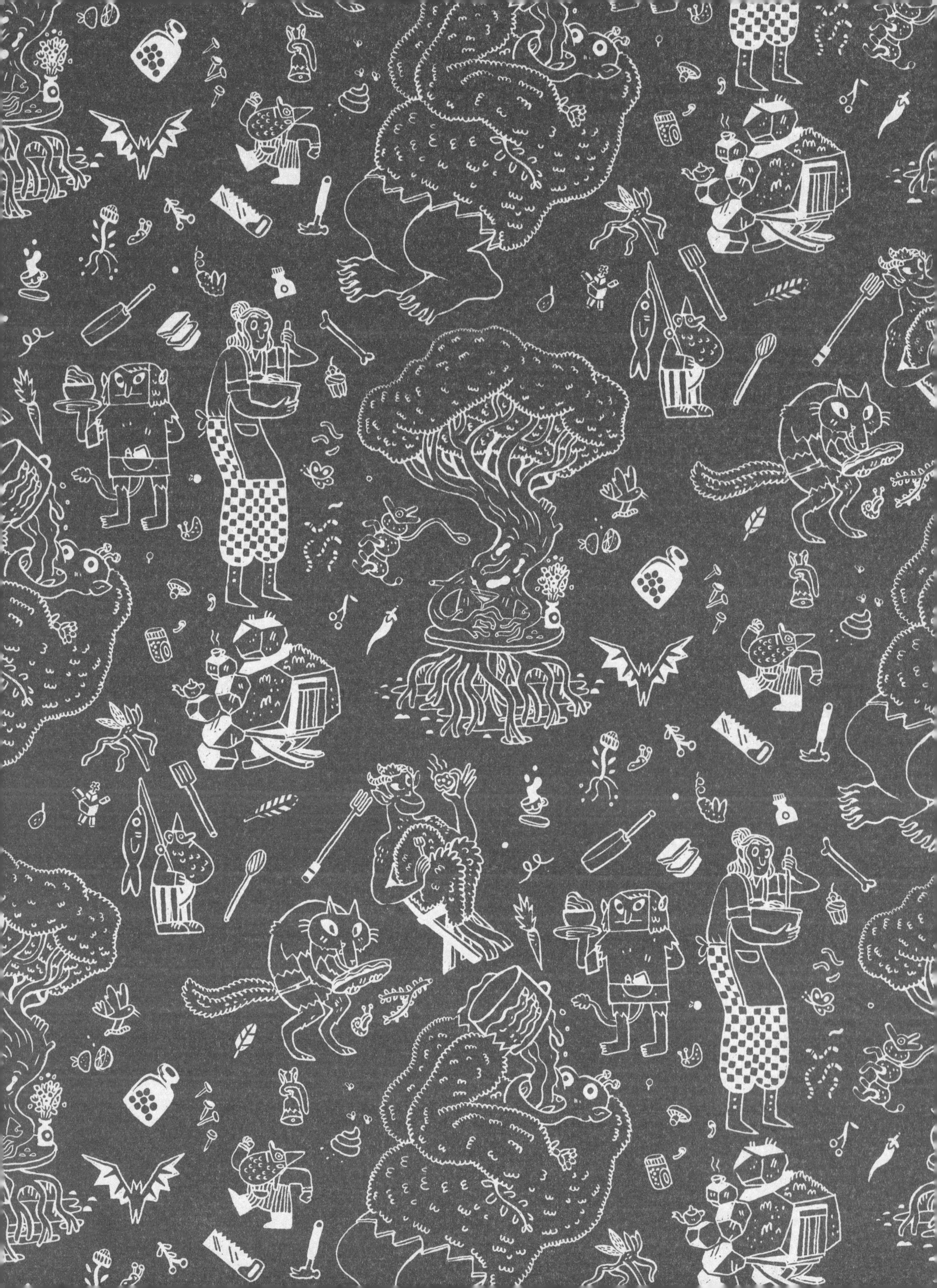